Two Hearts

A collection of love poems

Stan Rudge
18/1/24
Thank you

STAN RUDGE

Stan Rudge © Copyright 2023

The right of Stan Rudge to be identified as the author of this work has been asserted by him in accordance with the Copyright, Designs and Patents Act 1988.

All rights reserved.

No reproduction, copy or transmission of this publication may be made without express prior written permission. No paragraph of this publication may be reproduced, copied or transmitted except with express prior written permission or in accordance with the provisions of the Copyright Act 1956 (as amended). Any person who commits any unauthorised act in relation to this publication may be liable to criminal prosecution and civil claims for damage.

Cover image: Mayur Gala on www.unsplash.com
Photo on page 9: Sandy Millar on www.unsplash.com
Photo on page 39: Gary Howell-Jones

I've put together this collection of my love poems for you to enjoy. I've written them for people to read and share with their loved ones.

Writing the poems in this book was the best thing for me when I was suffering and it has helped me come to terms with a broken relationship. It has also helped me with my mental health which is something a lot of people struggle with.

I hope my poems will bring you comfort. So, grab a box of tissues, sit back and enjoy reading!

Stan Rudge

Contents

Love You	7
My Darling Wife	8
When You Went Away	10
Our Two Hearts	11
My Love	12
My Darling	13
You're Not Alone	14
My True Love	16
Summer Breeze	18
I Held You Close to My Heart	19
Friends	21
Wish You Knew	22
Just Wait	23
My Love for You	25
Make You Feel My Love	27
Queen of My Heart	28
Stars Tonight	30
My Heart	33
Faith in My Heart	34
Should I Stay?	36
Time to Say Goodbye	37
Steam Train	38
Our Two Hearts	41
For All Those Times	42
Goodbye	43
Forever Young	45
Walk Away	46

Love You

If I die young bury me with love
And send me away with your love
Lay me down on a bed of roses.

Old Lord make me in to a rainbow
So I can shine down on to my lover
So she will know I am safe with you.

Don't stand at my grave, I'm not there
I'm a thousand rainbows
Shining down on you.

Hear my cry in the wind saying
I love you always.

My Darling Wife

I see in your eyes
I see in your smiles
I've been looking at you forever
Yet I never saw you before
Your hands holding mine
Yet I wonder how I could have been so blind.

For the first time I am looking in your eyes
For the first time I'm seeing who you are
My loving wife.

I now understand what love is
Loving you my darling.

I love you forever.

When You Went Away

When you went away
I hated you so much
Yet my tears fill my broken heart
I led you on and that was my mistake
I learnt too late what I just lost
Your beautiful face and a gentle smile
I saw inside your eyes a beautiful child
I never thought the day would come
When you went away
My pain will follow me all my life.

I wish I could kiss her one last time
Please don't let her down or make her cry
I know I lost my one and only
Sometimes lovers say goodbye.

She's gone too far now
I know I have to just let her go
If I see her on the street
I'll just smile and say
I miss you and love you, my darling.

Our Two Hearts

Our love was meant to be
The kind of love to last
Always and forever
I want you here with me
To the end of time.

You should know you are
Always on my mind, in my heart
And in my soul
You're the meaning in my life
You bring feeling into my life
I have not felt for a long time.

You mean the world to me
I will love you today, tomorrow
And always.

Our two hearts are bound together by destiny.
I will still love you for the rest of my life.

My Love

I thought my life wouldn't matter
If we didn't stay together.

But maybe it was for the better
I don't want to live without you
I don't want to lose your love
I don't want to face my life alone
I could never make it through on my own.

I would never want to love anybody else
I don't want to lose your love
I just want to live my life with you, my love.

My Darling

You will fear no more
As my love will protect you always
You are in my heart, day and night
You are always in my thoughts
I sleep with you on my mind
My darling you are my queen of my heart
You are the life and soul of my heart
You are my darling, my heart.

You're Not Alone

I've seen you there
A silhouette in the moonlight
It seems you've given up on love
You used to be so happy when she was around.

But now you walk around in a cloak of darkness
Too blind to feel the light
Your heart may be broken
But you're not alone.

Tears of sorrow
Tears of sadness
Your heart is broken
For the loss of your lady
But you're not alone.

On the last night you were with her
Your heart was full of sorrow
And your eyes full of tears of sadness
But you saw her standing there in the bright light
Telling you
You're not alone.

My True Love

It's been a long and winding road
Through my darkest days
But I've faith in my heart
I'll find my true love.

I have known love before
I thought it would be no more
But my faith has taken me in a new direction
It is still strange as it seems to be
It's truly new to me.

I don't know what you want or do
But you make me think that you do
I'll always want you near me
I'll never give up on you, my dear.

You thrill me, you delight me
You please me, you excite me
You are all that I've been yearning for
I love you, I adore you

I lay my life on the line for you
I only want you.

And finally it's seems my faith has showed me
My lonely days are through
I've been waiting for you
My love.

Summer Breeze

Touch me gently
Like a summer breeze
Take me and show me your love
Just let the feeling grow
Touch my soul, you know how.

Let my body be
The velvet of the night
Let my soul touch you
Just let the feeling grow.

Let our love grow for each other
Let my love show you that
You are my soul, my heart, my love.

You will always be my love.

I Held You Close to My Heart

I held you close to my heart
I felt your heart beat
And I thought
I am free.

I image passing by my life, my love
In the mirror of your eyes
I see my love
In the reflections of my mind
I see my love
I hear the words I try to find, my love
I know I don't possess you
With all my love.

May the Lord bless you
You are still my life, my love
You will always be my one and only.

Friends

Some people say that I'm sometimes clueless and clumsy
Yet I know I've got friends that love me
And they all know just where I stand.

So if I make a big mistake
Or if I fall flat on my face
I know I'll be alright
Should anyone break my tender heart
I will cry those tears knowing
I will be fine
Because nothing changes who I am
Because I know I've got friends
Who love me.

Wish You Knew

I wish you just knew
How much I love you
I just got to see you wherever you are.
I wish upon a star that one day
You will see inside my heart
How much I love you.

All the words escape me when I'm with you
I'm so helpless when I look into your eyes
I wish you only knew the feeling
I've inside for you.

But you haven't got a clue
How much I love you
I wish you knew how much I love you
Honestly, I know it's silly
But one day you will see
How much I care and love you forever.

Just Wait

So there is no doubt you're beautiful, I'll say
I can see you're looking at me
You say you wanna get to know me better
I feel it when we're walking down this road
You're not just hard to talk to
But I don't want to lose this new thing
It could be a great thing.

Don't say you love me as I feel it too
Please realise you're pushing me away
I want to tell you to slow down
And show me a little love
I know you think you're showing me
That you love me and care for me
But right now babe, I'm not going there.

Just give me a minute as I'm not
Ready to commit my life
You're gonna have to try to be a good friend
Just tell me I'm worth the wait
And you love me.

My Love for You

If I had to live without you in my life
The days would be so empty
The nights would be so cold and
so long without you, my love.

I see we are made for each other So clearly now
I might have been in love before
But never felt this strong before.

I dream of the day we fell in love together
We both knew then we were made for each other.
I'll never ask for more than your love
The world where I love you
may change my whole life forever
But nothin's gonna change my love for you.
The road may not be so easy
but our love will lead the way.

Through the darkness and the light
Through the happy times and the sad times
Through richer, for poorer
Our love will shine through those hard times.
Nothing will change my love for you
As you are my love, my heart, my soul
So come with me and share my whole life

Make You Feel My Love

When the snow is blowing on to your face
And you have the whole world on your shoulders
I will offer you a warm embrace
If you let me love you.

When the evening shadows and the stars appear
There is no one there to dry the tears from your eyes
Let me hold you in my arms
If you let me love you
I know you haven't made your mind up
You know I would never do you wrong
No doubt in my mind where you belong
If only you would let me love you.

Queen of My Heart

I live through my darkest experience
Only to bask in your beauty
Your eyes that shine like sapphires
Your smile that brightens even my sadest experience.
I envy the wind that runs through your hair
That touches your lips I long to kiss.

You are my heart and soul, every feeling I know.
You are my black and my white,
my darkness and my light.
You take away my fear, the only one
I hold dear to my heart.
You cheer me up when times are blue,
when no one else has a clue.

Like a beautiful angel you touched my heart.
I want to care for you and always be there for you
I want to be your shoulder to cry on,
someone to rely upon
I want to carry you when you can't go on.
I'll always be there for you.

You will fear no more as my love will protect you
You are in my thoughts morning and evening
I sleep at nght with you on my mind.
My darling, you are the queen of my heart.

You are the life of my heart
You are the soul of my heart
You are the love of my heart
You are my darling, my heart.

Stars Tonight

The moon and stars are out tonight
Shining brightly on your smile.
Your love shines through your ruby eyes
As I whisper sweetly in your ear 'I love you'
And tell you how much I wish I could kiss your ruby lips
As I long to hold you in my arms.

As I'm lying in my bed I hear the ticking clock
And think of you
And remember the time we fell in love
on that starry night.

My Heart

I lost my heart to you a long time ago.
You made me feel like I've never
Been in love this way before.
You say I'm forever yours,
But you then walked out my door.

I will never love again until you're back
in my loving arms
I don't care how long it will take
Because love's never too far.
I know I might be crazy,
But when it comes to my heart,
I know I'll always love you.

Faith in My Heart

It's been a long and winding road
And my time is now finally near.
I can feel my time is changing in the wind right now.
There is nothing I can do
My heart is failing
But I've got faith in my heart...

That the faith in my heart will take me where I belong
I got faith to believe I'll no longer be in pain
I've got strength in my soul
That the love I leave behind will go on
And I'll reach the stars one last time.

It's been a long time coming.
Trying to find my way
I've been through the darkest time
Now I finally have my day to say goodbye.

But remember I've got faith in my heart
That the love we had will go on inside you
And one day we will meet again.

Should I Stay?

Should I stay?
We both know I would only be in your way.
I'm going but I will think of you
Every second of the day.
I will always love you.

I will remember every sweet memory we had
This is all I will take away with me, my love.
Goodbye, for now. Please don't cry.
We both agreed that I'm not what you want
But remember I'll always love you.

I know life will treat you with kindness
I know you will one day find
Everything you dreamed of.
And I hope one day you will find
All the joy and happiness you deserve.

I'll carry you always in my heart, my darling.
I love you always.

Time to Say Goodbye

It's time to say goodbye
We've been on a long and winding road
But our two hearts came together.

It's time to say goodbye.
My love for you will live on
In my heart, forever.
I've seen you grow from a beautiful seedling
To a beautiful red rose
But now it's time to say goodbye.

My feeling will burn in my broken heart for you.
It's now time to say goodbye.
Maybe we can stay as friends
Only time will tell.

It's time to say goodbye, my love.
I'll always love you and
Care for you, my love.

Goodbye, my love. I'll always love you.
Goodbye.

Steam Train

When our two hearts met for the first time
On that cold dark platform at Lydney Town
I knew my love for you would protect you
and guide you.

When we were on board I kissed your rosy lips
I knew then my love for you would last forever.

When I left you on the platform at Parkend
I looked back through the steam and
Saw your beautiful face shining through.

When I'm gone, my love
Just remember my love for you will live on
Forever in my heart.
Until we meet again, my love
Goodbye, my love.

Our Two Hearts

When our two hearts become one,
My love for you will protect and guide you.

When I'm gone my love for you
Will live on forever in my heart.
When you look up to the sky
I'll shine down on you.

When you are sad and feel you can't go on
Then that's when I'll be carrying you.
When you are alone and you think
no one is there for you
Then that's when I'll walk by your side.

My love for you will protect you
and guide you forever.

For All Those Times

For all those times I stood by you and loved you
For all the joy I brought to your life
For all the wrong that I made right for you
For all the love I saw in you
I never let you down.
You're the one that saw me
through the hardest of times.

You were my strength when I was weak
You were my voice when I couldn't speak
You were my eyes when I couldn't see anything
You lifted me up when I couldn't reach
You gave me faith to believe I could love again
But you still left me to be alone.

I now know I'll die alone
Without your love.
Goodbye, my love.

Goodbye

It's been a long and winding road
And it's time to say goodbye.
My love for you will live on
Forever in my heart.

There will always be an open door to my heart
When you make your mind up on
Who you want.

If this is goodbye then please let me down
And let me go.
One day you'll find your true happiness.
Until then, goodbye my love, goodbye.

And if I see you walking down the street
I'll look away, but my heart
It will be calling you and saying
I miss you my love.

Forever Young

May the Lord be with you.
Down every winding road you roam
May the Sunshine and true happiness surround you.
As you're far from home
May you grow to be proud.
And be courageous and be brave.
As in my heart you'll always stay
Forever Young.

May good fortune be with you.
May your guiding light be with you
As my heart will remain
Forever Young.

As you finally fly away
I hope that I've served you well.
As all my wisdom of my lifetime
Will guide you forever.
Whatever road you may choose.
I'll be right behind you.
Forever Young.

Walk Away

My eyes look beyond your beauty
That lies before me.
But my lips, say goodbye to her
Though you know she adores you.
If you know what's good for you
Just stand up and walk away
As you've got to stop loving her today.

You'll save yourself a lot of pain
As she belongs to someone else
and that will not change
But it's easy to say just walk away.
But when you lose your heart to her
that's what really hurts.
I wish I could find a way to walk away
That won't tear my heart apart
That's the hardest part.

Why is life so hard that you can't have what you Love?
I'll try and keep a straight face
while inside me is crying out for you.
I'll try and walk away but knowing
My broken heart will be calling you
And saying I love you.

Printed in Great Britain
by Amazon